To Carmen & Bootz
and all the other little people and furry
friends that continue to inspire us!
GY & SP

Dear Gus

Enjoy your book!

Genevieve

A 'JAJAJA' BOOK

First published in Great Britain in 2018 by JaJaJa Books

Text copyright © 2018 Genevieve Yusuf
Illustration copyright © 2018 Shermain Philip

Design by Karen Clark

The author's and the illustrator's moral rights have been asserted.

ISBN 978-0-9569411-7-6

Printed in Great Britain

www.jajaja-books.com

Deep in the heart of the olive groves of Sevilla...

...in the heat of the Spanish **sol**, a farmer found a tiny black and brown puppy, all alone and curled up in a shady spot.

No one knew how she had got there, so he picked her up, put her in a box and took her to the nearest rescue **centro**. Little did the farmer know that there was something **especial** about this puppy...

"Una cachorra," he said as he passed the box over at the centre. It was full of **perros** needing new homes. Small ones, big ones, yappy ones and shy ones.

The little puppy felt tired and found a small knitted blanket in the corner to cuddle up on.

That afternoon a young girl called Eliana came in with her parents. She was sad as they were moving back to England. Her **madre** had promised she could choose a little puppy to take back with her.

She said they could give a puppy a new start in **Inglaterra**, and it would be Eliana's new friend.

Eliana looked at all the lonely **perros** in their cages and wanted to take them all home. Eliana had a big heart and was a very kind little girl. She stopped by the cage of a tiny black and brown puppy. The **cachorra** looked up at her and tilted its head to one side. Its sweet furry face and big hazel **ojos** were beautiful.

It had scrappy hair that needed a good comb. Eliana had found her puppy. She would name her after her favourite aunty and call her Vivi.

When they opened the cage, Vivi came running out and straight into Eliana's arms, so she gave her a big cuddle and tickled Vivi's tummy. Vivi in return licked Eliana's chin.

From that day on the two of them became very best **amigas**. Eliana loved Vivi and Vivi loved Eliana.

But Eliana didn't know Vivi's big **secreto**. Vivi the Spanish rescue dog had extra-special powers and was in fact a...

And so the **aventuras** began...

SUPERDOG!!

It was a cold, blustery morning in England and Vivi had jumped on Eliana's bed as usual and licked her face **tres** times.
Uno, dos, tres!

"Vivi, STOP!" Eliana giggled as Vivi jumped all over her bed covers excitedly. "OK, if you stop I will take you for a walk."

Eliana got dressed and put on her warm coat, woolly **guantes** and pom pom hat. Vivi waited impatiently for her lead to be put on. Jump, jump, **saltar!** Vivi loved going for walks. And why did she love walks? Because it was her chance to see if anybody would need saving in the big wide world out there. Vivi definitely took her superdog status seriously.

As the two of them made their way down Ticklebrick Avenue Vivi took note of everything around her and logged it in her head.

'**Un árbol**, a tree looking a bit wobbly in the wind by the **casa** of Mr and Mrs Clayton.'

'A suspicious-looking **hombre** hanging around the bikes by the **supermercado**.'

"Come on, Vivi," pleaded Eliana. "It's too windy and cold to be investigating everything and I need to pop in the supermarket, so be a good girl and stay here on your lead." Eliana wrapped Vivi's lead around a post outside the shop and Vivi put her **nariz** in the air. She was sniffing for trouble. All seemed well.

On their return Vivi saw the Clayton's **gato**, Edward, sitting on a fence and licking his paws. "**Hola, Eduardo**," Vivi barked across the road. "You look very **contento**."

"Hey there, Vivi. Yeah, I'm thinking of taking Katya out tonight so I'm pretty happy."

"Well be careful with this **viento**, Eduardo, it's going to be even windier tonight."

"Will do, Vivi, thanks for the concern." Edward nodded and continued to casually lick his paws.

Vivi seemed satisfied that Eduardo had listened to her word of warning and carried on walking and watching, **andando** and watching. Eliana tugged her towards home. "Vivi, you mustn't bark at the cats!" Vivi chuckled to herself. These humans really had no idea how we communicated.

The two of them spent the rest of the **día** in the warm. Snacking, sitting in front of the fire and playing some hide-the-treat games in the kitchen. The **viento** outside was howling and as they went up to bed at eight, Vivi pretended to cuddle up at the end of Eliana's **cama**.

...But Vivi was on high alert. She didn't know how she had inherited these super **poderes** or when she had first found out about them.

She just knew she was **SÚPER!**

At 10 o'clock she sniffed Eliana's face and made sure she was fast asleep.

She clipped on her cape azul that was hidden under the wardrobe and squeezed through the old cat flap that was still in the back door, making sure not to make any ruido that might wake the familia.

She made her way down the side alley and onto the main street. There, Vivi began her patrol.

The wind whistled past her flappy ears and sent her **capa** high into the air, but Vivi didn't mind, she was out to protect the people of Ticklebrick **Avenida**.

After a couple of **horas**, braving it in the wind, with her fur all ruffled and her paws tired, she noticed the feeble **árbol** from earlier bending dangerously in the wind

...but what was that on a branch...Eduardo!!

Vivi raced up the street to see what could be done, but as she did the tall tree took one final blast in the wind and started to **caer** over into a garden.

Vivi ran to the site and managed to use her super **fuerte** body to redirect the tree onto the lawn, narrowly missing a **casa**! **Phew**, she thought, I've saved the day again.

But hold on ...where was Eduardo?? Vivi called out:

"Eduardo, *¿dónde estás?* "

In the distance, she could hear a faint cat cry. Vivi looked around and could see Eduardo trapped by a fallen wall and the spiky branches of the tree in the corner of the garden.

"Don't worry, **no te preocupes**, Eduardo, **me voy**, I'm commmmmming!!". Vivi ran up to the **árbol**, summoned up her super **rápido** paw power and started to dig.

Vivi ran back through the tunnel, taking Eduardo with her. He clung onto her **capa** with all his might and eventually they reached the other side.

"Gracias, my friend,"
muchísimas gracias,
Eduardo said with relief,
licking his fur of all the dirt.
"You saved my life!"
"No **problema**, Eduardo,
my **amigo**. All in a night's
work! What were you doing
up there anyway?"

Eduardo looked sheepish.
"Well, I was coming to take Katya out,
but as I got to her door, her owners
came out and seemed really mad at
me. The old man chased me up the
tree, I didn't know where else to go."

"Some people," sighed Vivi. "Anyway, I need to go **dormir**, I'm feeling pretty tired. See you soon, Eduardo."
"Sure. Thanks again, Vivi."

She cuddled up on Eliana's bed and wondered what **aventuras** she would have tomorrow night.

Do you want to sound like...

VIVI

THE SPANISH SUPERDOG?

Then just follow our vocab list with pronunciation guides below:

Sol Sol - *Sun*

Centro Thentroh - *Centre*

Especial Espethyal - *Special*

Una cachorra Katchorrra - *A puppy*

Perros Perrrrohs **(roll your rrrrrrs!)** - *Dogs*

Madre Madray - *Mother*

Inglaterra Inglatairrra - *England*

Amigas Ameegas - *Friends*

Secreto Sehkretoh - *Secret*

Aventuras Abentouras - *Adventures*

Uno Oono - *One*

Dos Dos - *Two*

Tres Tress - *Three*

Guantes Gwantez - *Gloves*

Saltar Saltahr - *to Jump*

Un árbol Oon ahrbol - *A tree*

Casa Kassa - *House*

Hombre Ombreh - *Man*

Supermercado Soopermerkadoh - *Supermarket*

Nariz Nareeth - *Nose*

Gato Gatoh - *Cat*

Hola Ohla - *Hello*

Contento Kontentoh - *Happy*

Viento Beeyentoh - *Wind*

Andando Andandoh - *Walking*

Día Deeya - *Day*

Cama Kama - *Bed*

Poderes Podairess - *Powers*

Súper Soopair - *Super*

Azul Athool - *Blue*

Ruido *Rooweedoh* - Noise
Familia *Fameeleeyah* - Family
Capa *Kappa* - Cape
Avenida *Abeneeda* - Avenue
Horas *Oras* - Hours
Árbol *Ahrbol* - Tree
Caer *Kayair* - to Fall
Fuerte *Fwairteh* - Strong
¿Dónde estás? *Donday estass* - Where are you?
No te preocupes *No teh prayocoopes* - Don't worry
Me voy *Meh boy* - I'm coming
Rápido *Rapeedoh* - Quick
Más rápido *Mass rappeedoh* - Quicker
Muchísimas *Moochiseemass* - Many
Gracias *Gratheeyass* - Thanks
Problema *Problema* - Problem
Amigo *Ameego* - Friend
Dormir *Dormeer* - to Sleep
Hasta la próxima *Asta la proxeema* - Until next time

What do you think 'VOLAR' means?

(Clue... Vivi can do this when she has her cape on!)

JaJaJa Books

To find more titles by JaJaJa Books go to
www.jajaja-books.com

Printed in Poland
by Amazon Fulfillment
Poland Sp. z o.o., Wrocław